THE ADVENTURES OF EL CIPITÍO

LAS AVENTURAS DEL CIPITÍO

Written by RANDY JURADO ERTLL

Illustrated by BILLY BURGOS

Published in the United States of America by
ERTLL PUBLISHERS

WWW.RANDYJURADOERTLL.COM

Illustrations by Billy Burgos

ISBN 978-0-9909929-6-7 (pbk.)

ISBN 978-0-9909929-8-1 (hardcover)

ISBN 978-0-9909929-7-4 (ebk.)

First edition 2018

Printed in the United States of America

1 2 3 4 5 6 7 8 9 10

My name is ____

I AM DETERMINED TO DREAM BIG!

Date: ____

Signature: ____

❧❀❧

Mi nombre es ____

¡ME COMPROMETO A SOÑAR EN GRANDE!

Fecha: ____

Firma: ____

CONTENTS

I have to leave my home, my family, my friends, and my favorite foods: los guineos majonchos, tamales de elote, tamales pisques, pupusas, el fresco de chan, y la horchata. I am leaving my native country El Salvador to seek a better future in the United States. My dream is to also bring peace to my small native country.

Tengo que dejar mi hogar, mi familia, mis amigos y mis comidas favoritas: los guineos majonchos, los tamales de elote, los tamales pisques, las pupusas, el fresco de chan y la horchata. Me voy de El Salvador a buscar un futuro mejor en los Estados Unidos. Mi sueño es traer paz a mi pequeño país natal.

I will miss you mother with all my heart and soul. You have protected me and fed me. I will also miss my grandparents who worked the land all their lives. They grew coffee, watermelons, sesame seeds, and many other fruits and vegetables that were sold in el mercado.

Te extrañaré madre con toda mi alma. Me has protegido y me has alimentado. También extrañaré a mis abuelos que trabajaron la tierra toda su vida. Cosecharon café, sandías, semillas de ajonjolí, y muchas otras frutas y verduras que se venden en el mercado.

El Cipitío migrates through Guatemala. This is where our ancestors worshipped and lived – I am so proud of my indigenous roots. After thousands of years only a few temple ruins remain, but our culture and history run through our veins. We cannot deny our Mayan and Aztec roots; we need to know our history. El Salvador, Guatemala, and Mexico have beautiful, kind, and generous people.

⊛⊷⧈⊶⊗

El Cipitío emigra a través de Guatemala. Aquí es donde adoraron y vivieron nuestros antepasados. Estoy muy orgulloso de mis raíces indígenas. Después de miles de años, solo quedan unas pocas ruinas de los templos, pero su cultura e historia corren por nuestras venas. No podemos negar nuestras raíces mayas y aztecas; necesitamos conocer nuestro origen. En El Salvador, Guatemala y México viven hermosas personas, amables y generosas.

Holy Father please protect my family in El Salvador and please help me to cross Mexico safely. I only brought with me a few colones, some semillas de marañon, and my favorite Chapulin Colorado picture. My dream is to cross Mexico and reach the United States, so I can work and become a great role model for my community.

Padre Santo, por favor, proteja a mi familia en El Salvador y ayúdame a cruzar México de manera segura. Nada más traje algunos colones, algunas semillas de marañón y mi foto favorita del Chapulín Colorado. Mi sueño es cruzar México y llegar a los Estados Unidos para poder trabajar y convertirme en un inmigrante modelo para mi comunidad.

I miss my family. Some teachers don't understand why I cannot speak English. Some teachers tell me that my family and I will be arrested and deported. I am not a criminal! We are children who left our home countries to save our own lives and to find a better future. I will graduate from elementary school, middle school, and high school. I will attend great colleges and universities. I will prepare myself to become a well-rounded leader who can speak with the poor and the rich, and treat all with dignity and respect.

Extraño a mi familia. Algunos maestros no entienden porque no puedo hablar inglés. Algunos maestros me dicen que mi familia y yo vamos a ser arrestados y deportados. ¡Pero nosotros no somos criminales! Muchos somos niños que abandonamos nuestros países de origen para salvar nuestras propias vidas y encontrar un futuro mejor. Aprenderé inglés y luego me graduaré de la escuela primaria, de la secundaria y la preparatoria. Asistiré a grandes colegios y universidades. Me prepararé muy bien para convertirme en un líder que pueda hablar con los pobres y los ricos, y tratar a todos con dignidad y respeto.

We are not aliens – we are human beings who deserve respect. We can no longer remain invisible. We need to become more knowledgeable in order to empower our own community. We have to fight for civil rights and human rights for all human beings. Knowledge is power.

⊷⊶⧈⊷⊶

No somos extranjeros, somos seres humanos que merecemos respeto. Ya no podemos permanecer en las sombras, de una manera invisible. Debemos darle fuerza y poder a nuestra comunidad. Tenemos que luchar por los derechos de todos los seres humanos. El conocimiento es poder.

R
P
BL CK
NO HUMAN
BEING IS
ILLEGAL
DON
SHO

I will create jobs for everyone – so all can afford rent and food, and pay taxes and the bills – los biles. I have sacrificed and struggled by working hard as a paletero. Now I don't want to just sell paletas, I want us to dream big. That is why I ran for mayor and became the first indigenous mayor of a major U.S. city – Los Angeles. We have to follow our dreams and make our goals a reality.

❧❦❧

Crearé trabajos para todos, para que cada persona pueda pagar el alquiler de casa y la comida, así como los impuestos y las facturas; es decir, los biles. Me he sacrificado y luchado porque he trabajado muy duro como paletero. Pero ya no quiero solo vender paletas, sino soñar en grande. Es por eso que me postulé para alcalde y gané, y me convertí en el primer mandatario indígena de una importante ciudad de los Estados Unidos, Los Angeles. Tenemos que seguir soñando y hacer que nuestros propósitos se hagan realidad.

13

Never let your dreams evaporate. Make your dreams and goals a reality. If a dream does not come to fruition, then you move on to the next dream or goal, and make it a reality. Failures and mistakes do not define your life. Failures and mistakes make you strong and resilient. Never lose your imagination and freedom to dream big!

❈❈❈

Nunca dejes que tus sueños se evaporen. Haz que las aspiraciones de tus metas se hagan realidad. Si un sueño no se realizara, esto no significaría que has fracasado. Con persistencia lograrás hacer tus sueños una realidad. Las fallas y los errores no definen tu vida. Las fallas y los errores te hacen fuerte y resistente. Nunca pierdas tu imaginación y libertad para soñar en grande!

I now represent the dreams of the indigenous, Aztec and Mayan people – thank you for electing me as your first indigenous, bilingual, U.S. President. I will provide jobs, a quality education, free healthcare for all. I will continue to fight for clean air and water. I will protect our communities from pollution. I will build homes for the poor and we will feed all hungry children, not just those in the United States, but those in developing countries that need our help. My motto is 'let's build schools, not prisons.'

Ahora represento los sueños de los pueblos mayas y aztecas. Gracias por elegirme como su primer presidente indígena, bilingüe y estadounidense. Proporcionaré empleos, una educación de calidad y atención médica gratuita para todos. Continuaré luchando para tener aire y agua limpios. Protegeré nuestras comunidades de la contaminación. Construiré hogares para los pobres y alimentaremos a todos los niños necesitados, no solo a los que viven en los Estados Unidos, sino también aquellos que viven en países en vías de desarrollo, y que necesitan de nuestra ayuda. Mi lema es: 'construyamos escuelas, no prisiones.'

PRESIDENT

Cipotes y Cipotas, a bailar La Bala, se ha dicho!
"La bala, a bailar la bala y la tienes que bailar
porque si tú no la bailas te la pueden disparar…"

Author

RANDY JURADO ERTLL is an award winning published author, educator, and newspaper columnist. He has also served as executive director for non-profit organizations focused on education and environmental issues.

Ertll served as a communications director for a Congressional member on Capitol Hill in Washington, D.C. He has published numerous opinion columns in newspapers and magazines such as the Los Angeles Times, USA Today, La Opinión, Daily News, La Prensa Grafica, San Diego Union-Tribune, Atlanta Journal-Constitution, Houston Chronicle, The Progressive and The American Interest magazines. He has been interviewed by networks such as NPR, CNN, PBS, Univisión, and Telemundo. He is an alumnus of Occidental College where he obtained the prestigious 2015 Alumni Seal Award for Service to the Community and obtained his master's degree from Azusa Pacific University. He has published the following books: Hope in Times of Darkness: A Salvadoran American Experience, Esperanza en Tiempos de Oscuridad: La Experiencia de un Salvadoreño Americano, The Life of an Activist: In the Frontlines 24/7, The Lives and Times of El Cipitío, La Vida Y Los Tiempos Del Cipitío, In The Struggle: Chronicles, and The Adventures of El Cipitío. Please visit his web site at WWW.RANDYJURADOERTLL.COM

Illustrator

BILLY BURGOS is an Illustrator/Designer/Poet from Los Angeles. His poetry has been featured in both Anthologies and Literary Journals and Zines. His vivid paintings of some of Los Angeles most interesting poets called The Faces of Poetry is a traveling gallery/poetry exhibit which has been featured in both art journals as well as KCET. His artwork has been featured at The Mike Kelly Gallery in Venice, California as well as at Ave 50 Performance Gallery in Highland Park. Burgos has also designed book cover illustrations for numerous poets and writers. His first full length collection of poetry called Eulogy to an Unknown Tree is out now and it is published by Writ Large Press.

Ertll and Burgos are childhood friends. They both want to share Central American culture, art and literature with the world.

* 9 7 8 0 9 9 0 9 9 2 9 6 7 *